FEB 13

THE
Icecutter's
DAUGHTER

Books by Tracie Peterson

www.traciepeterson.com

House of Secrets
A Slender Thread
Where My Heart Belongs

LAND OF THE LONE STAR
Chasing the Sun
Touching the Sky
Taming the Wind

BRIDAL VEIL ISLAND*
To Have and To Hold
To Love and Cherish
To Honor and Trust

SONG OF ALASKA
Dawn's Prelude
Morning's Refrain
Twilight's Serenade

STRIKING A MATCH
Embers of Love
Hearts Aglow
Hope Rekindled

ALASKAN QUEST
Summer of the Midnight Sun
Under the Northern Lights
Whispers of Winter
Alaskan Quest (3 in 1)

BRIDES OF GALLATIN COUNTY
A Promise to Believe In
A Love to Last Forever
A Dream to Call My Own

THE BROADMOOR LEGACY*
A Daughter's Inheritance
An Unexpected Love
A Surrendered Heart

BELLS OF LOWELL*
Daughter of the Loom
A Fragile Design
These Tangled Threads

LIGHTS OF LOWELL*
A Tapestry of Hope
A Love Woven True
The Pattern of Her Heart

DESERT ROSES
Shadows of the Canyon
Across the Years
Beneath a Harvest Sky

HEIRS OF MONTANA
Land of My Heart
The Coming Storm
To Dream Anew
The Hope Within

LADIES OF LIBERTY
A Lady of High Regard
A Lady of Hidden Intent
A Lady of Secret Devotion

RIBBONS OF STEEL**
Distant Dreams
A Hope Beyond
A Promise for Tomorrow

RIBBONS WEST**
Westward the Dream
Separate Roads
Ties That Bind

WESTWARD CHRONICLES
A Shelter of Hope
Hidden in a Whisper
A Veiled Reflection

YUKON QUEST
Treasures of the North
Ashes and Ice
Rivers of Gold

*with Judith Miller   **with Judith Pella